My First Bow

Written by Robert H. Jacobs, Jr.
Illustrated by Jared Beckstrand & Mark Swan

A Little Sportsman Book, Copyright © 2008 Little Sportsman Inc..

First Edition and First Printing

10 9 8 7 6 5 4 3 2 1

Printed in the United States of America.

ISBN-10: 0-9800976-7-3
ISBN-13: 978-0-9800976-7-2

Building a Better
Generation of Sportsmen!

Well, I've finally saved enough money to buy my first bow and arrows. I've wanted my own bow for a very long time.

Sometimes I daydream about being an archer, just like Robin Hood.

My Dad and I went to the store and picked out a bow that fits me perfectly. My new bow is just like my Dad's, only smaller. It's called a compound bow. It is very important that your bow fits you just right.

Most archers use compound bows these days. This is called modern archery. Compound bows usually have wheels or pulleys on the limbs. They can shoot an arrow very fast and far.

In the Wild West, Indians used bows and arrows too. They were very good hunters.

They would hunt animals like deer and bison. They had to be good hunters or they went hungry.

The bows that Indians used were called traditional bows. They were usually made of wood and string.

Some people still use traditional bows.

To become good with any kind of bow takes a lot of practice. I'm going to shoot my bow every day because it's so much fun.

You need to be careful with whatever kind of bow you use. Archery is very safe and fun if you simply follow a few safety rules.

It's important to find a good instructor. A good instructor will teach you the right way to hold your bow and how to stand while shooting.

Without a good instructor you can develop bad shooting habits. An instructor will also teach you safety. My dad is my instructor.

Never shoot your bow inside a house. Bows are not toys. They can be dangerous if you become careless with them.

You should have an adult with you whenever you practice shooting your bow.

**Never point a bow at people or pets.
Not even a toy bow.**

Only point your bow at the target you plan on shooting. If you become careless, accidents can happen.

Never shoot an arrow straight up in the air. This is very dangerous.

You never know where the arrow will land and someone could get hurt.

Always make sure you have a good, safe target to shoot your bow at.

Do not shoot if you do not know what's behind your target. Never shoot towards homes or buildings.

Do not ever dry-fire a bow. Dry-firing means to shoot a bow without an arrow in it.

This can break a bow very easily. You can also get hurt this way.

Always use arrows that are long enough for your bow. If the arrow is too short you can become injured.

Always check your arrows before you shoot them. Do not use an arrow that is cracked or broken. This can also injure you.

Take good care of your bow and it will last a long time. Keep your bowstring waxed and it will also last a long time.

Always replace your bowstring when it starts to get worn out. You do not want to break a string. It can damage your bow.

When I get good enough with my bow, I'm going hunting with my dad. He is a good hunter and will teach me all that I need to know about hunting.

At first I'm going to hunt small game like rabbits and squirrels. They are delicious.

When I get bigger, I am going to go deer hunting. I'll probably get a bigger deer than my dad will.

Maybe someday I will even get to hunt bison like the Indians did. That would be fun.

I am going to go practice shooting my new bow now. Archery is just so much fun. You should give it a try. I think you will like it.